# My First Day of School

ISBN 0-8249-4198-5

Published by CandyCane Press, an imprint of Ideals Publications
a division of Guideposts
535 Metroplex Drive, Suite 250
Nashville, Tennessee 37211
www.idealspublications.com

Text copyright © 2001 by Ideals Publications, a division of Guideposts
Art copyright © 2001 by Meredith Johnson

Color scans by Precision Color Graphics, Franklin, WI
Printed and bound in Mexico by RR Donnelley & Sons


Library of Congress Cataloging-in-Publication Data
Skarmeas, Nancy J.
        My first day of school / illustrated by Meredith Johnson;
written by Nancy Skarmeas.
        p. cm.
        Summary: Daniel liked preschool just fine, but he is not so
sure he wants to go to kindergarten.
        ISBN 0-8249-4198-5 (alk. paper)
        [1. Kindergarten–Fiction. 2. First day of school–Fiction. 3.
Schools–Fiction.] I. Johnson, Meredith, ill. II. Title.
        PZ7.S62565 My 2000
        [E]–dc21                                        00-049416

JP
SKARMEAS
[30]P. il,
col. il,

Art Director, Eve DeGrie
Copy Editor, Amy Johnson

For G.T.M

# My First Day of School

Written by Nancy Skarmeas    Illustrated by Meredith Johnson

CandyCane Press

An imprint of
Ideals Publications, a division of Guideposts
Nashville, Tennessee

Daniel was five years old. He lived with his mother, his father, his baby sister, two dogs, and a parakeet.

Daniel rode his bike in the driveway and played in his sandbox. He went to swimming lessons on Wednesdays and to his Gramma's house every Friday afternoon. On Mondays he played with his friends Nathan and Emma. After lunch Daniel went to the library for story time.

Last year, every Tuesday and Thursday morning, Daniel went to preschool. They had gym time and snack time and story time. They painted and colored. They made windsocks and hand puppets. They even did a volcano experiment. Mrs. Riley, his teacher, wasn't angry when the water spilled all over the floor.

Daniel loved preschool. But now Mom said he was ready for kindergarten. Daniel wasn't sure about kindergarten.

Everywhere Daniel went, grownups talked about kindergarten. One day, Mrs. Gungle, who lived on the farm across the road, was outside milking her goats.

"Kindergarten!" she shouted. "You must be excited to
ride the big school bus all by yourself!"

Daniel didn't answer. He wondered about the school bus.
Where would he sit? How would he know when to get off?

At the library, Miss Karla, the children's librarian, smiled at Daniel.

"You will love kindergarten!" she said. "Soon you'll be reading all by yourself!"

Daniel didn't say anything. He knew his ABC's, but he couldn't read. What if the kindergarten teacher asked him to read? Anyway, he liked Mommy to read to him.

Everyone else seemed excited, but Daniel wasn't sure about kindergarten.

When Daniel, Mom, and the baby went to the pond to swim, Mrs. Peters asked Mom who Daniel's kindergarten teacher would be.

"Mrs. Soucy," said Mom.

"Terrific!" said Mrs. Peters. "My boys had Mrs. Soucy and they loved her!"

But Daniel wasn't sure. He liked Mrs. Riley. She had pretty red hair and she always listened to him. When Daniel felt sad, Mrs. Riley always knew to get his stuffed penguin from his cubby for him to hug.

Cousin Pete had been to kindergarten. He told Daniel that kindergarten was not like preschool.

"You have to walk down a long, dark hallway to the bathroom," Pete said. "And you can't ever talk unless you raise your hand."

Pete said that kindergarten was in a huge school and all the doors looked alike. One time, Pete told him, a boy couldn't find his room and got lost. The teachers didn't find him until after lunch.

Mom said, "Pete is exaggerating."

Daniel didn't know what "exaggerating" was. He did know that he didn't want to go to kindergarten.

Mom talked a lot about kindergarten too. She told Daniel about all the new friends he would make. One day at the grocery store, they met another mother and little boy.

"This is Nicholas," Mom said to Daniel. "He is going to be in your kindergarten class!"

Daniel didn't say hello. He liked his old friends. He didn't want new friends.

At swimming lessons, Mom spoke to the teacher, Mr. Ott. "We can't come to lessons anymore on Wednesdays," she said. "Kindergarten starts next week!"

"Daniel," said Mr. Ott, "since you are starting kindergarten, Mommy can come swim with the baby."

Daniel didn't want Mom to swim with the baby. He began to wonder. Would Mom take the baby to story time and to the park and to Gramma's while he was in kindergarten? Would they have so much fun that they would forget about him? No, Daniel thought, I had better not go to kindergarten.

The night before the first day of kindergarten, Daniel's mother tucked him into bed. She picked out a book to read.

"I can't believe you will start kindergarten tomorrow," she said. "You're such a big boy."

Just as Mom began to read, Daniel's sister started crying.

"I'll be back in a minute," Mom said.

Daniel closed his eyes and tried not to think about tomorrow. He didn't want to go to kindergarten. He wanted to stay home with Mommy. He didn't want to ride the bus or learn to read. He didn't want new friends or a new teacher. He didn't want to be a big boy. He wanted everything to stay just the same.

When Mom came back, Daniel was fast asleep. She kissed his head and stayed for awhile watching him sleep.

In the morning, Daniel ate breakfast quietly.

"Mom," he finally said, "I don't think I am ready for kindergarten."

"Well," said Mom gently, "why don't you try it for just one day and see how it goes?"

"If I don't like it, can I never, ever go back?" Daniel asked.

"Let's try one day," Mom said, "and then we'll see."

After breakfast, Daniel, his mother, and the baby walked to the end of the driveway to wait for the bus.

Daniel was surprised when the bus pulled up. It wasn't the same big yellow school bus he'd seen bringing the big kids home every afternoon. It was a small yellow school bus, and inside were other kids just his size.

Daniel felt a little bit like crying, but he didn't. He gave his mother a hug and a kiss.

"I love you," she whispered. "Have fun!"

Daniel carried his backpack to a
seat in the front, right next to Nicholas,
the boy from the grocery store.

"I'm going to kindergarten,"
Daniel said quietly.

"Me too," said Nicholas.

Daniel looked out the window and
waved good-bye to Mom until he
couldn't see her anymore.

Then Daniel showed Nicholas the
superheroes on his backpack and
Nicholas told Daniel that his birthday
was in eight days.

In just a few minutes, the driver
said, "Here we are!"

The bus drove into the school parking lot. Daniel felt a little scared. The school was bigger than his preschool. The bus door opened, and there was Mrs. Soucy.

"Welcome to kindergarten!" she said with a great big smile.

Mrs. Soucy led the children into the classroom. She showed them where to hang their backpacks.

The classroom looked a lot like Daniel's preschool. There were painting easels, round tables with kid-sized chairs, big soft pillows, and shelves full of books. And the bathroom door was right inside the classroom.

The kids sat in a circle around Mrs. Soucy. She called their names. They sang a song and she told them about all the things they'd do in kindergarten. Mrs. Soucy said they would practice letters and numbers. They would take field trips to a science museum and to the zoo.

Daniel painted a picture for Mom and wrote his name on it all by himself. Then they had a snack and played on the playground. There was a giant wooden castle with four different slides.

Inside, after Mrs. Soucy read them a story, Daniel was surprised to hear her say that it was time to go home.

Daniel sat with Nicholas on the bus ride home. When the bus stopped at Daniel's house, Mom was sitting on the grass next to the driveway. Daniel grabbed his backpack, said good-bye to Nicholas, and ran down the steps.

"I missed you," Mom said. "How was kindergarten?"

"Oh, Mom," Daniel said, "I think I will go back again tomorrow!"

"Are you sure?" she asked.

"Yes," said Daniel, " I am sure."